Geejay the Hero

Adèle Geras

Illustrated by

Tony Ross

A Dell Yearling Book

Published by
Dell Yearling
an imprint of
Random House Children's Books
a division of Random House, Inc.
New York

First American Edition 2003
First published in Great Britain by Young Corgi Books, Transworld Publishers Ltd,
a division of the Random House Group Ltd, in 1998

Illustrations by arrangement with Transworld Publishers Ltd,
a division of the Random House Group Ltd

Visit us on the Web! www.randomhouse.com/kids
Educators and librarians, for a variety of teaching tools, visit us at
www.randomhouse.com/teachers

ISBN: 0-440-41817-8 (pbk.) ISBN: 0-385-90082-1 (lib. bdg.)
Printed in the United States of America
April 2003
10 9 8 7 6 5 4 3 2 1
OPM

Contents

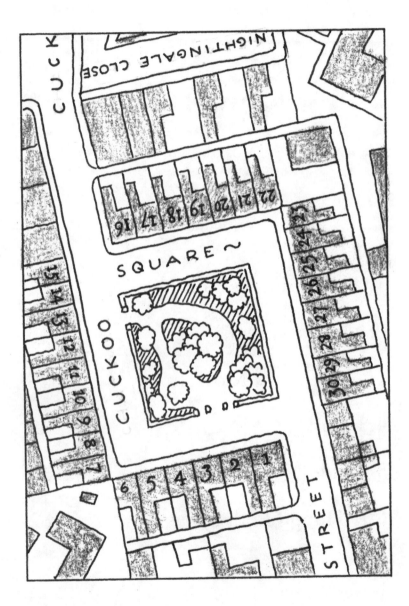

1.
The Haunted House

Once upon a time . . . that's the way all the very best stories begin. Wendy says so. She loves stories more than anything because, she says, they are full of wonders and marvels, adventures and magic. They tell us about a world that is more exciting than the real world. They are full of heroes and heroines, witches and

1

dragons, and they sometimes have ghosts in them. Wendy likes spooky stories best of all. She is eight years old, and she's my favorite human. It's her bed I sleep on when I rest from my work of hunting and roaming.

"Guess what?" Wendy whispered to me one day when we were playing in the garden. "I think the house next door is haunted. Doesn't it look haunted to you?"

Wendy has a habit of seeing ghosts everywhere. The dressing gown on the back of her door was one, and so was the wind, making the curtains blow in at the windows. The haunted house, No. 1 Cuckoo Square, stood on the corner of Peacock Street. It had been empty for a long time, and the paintwork was peeling. The windows were covered in spiderwebs, and ivy grew all over the walls at the back. When Wendy told her mother what she had told me, her mother, Angela, said: "What a lot of nonsense! Of course it's not haunted. You know perfectly well that ghosts are only in stories. It's just a bit neglected, that's all."

"You're not to go inside," said Nigel, Wendy's father. "Even though it's not haunted. Old houses can be very dangerous."

"What sort of dangerous?" Wendy wanted to know. She is as curious as any cat.

"Loose floorboards sort of dangerous," said Nigel. "Broken stairs sort of dangerous. Fall over and break your ankle sort of dangerous."

"Oh," said Wendy. "How boring!"

"Sorry, I'm sure!" Nigel smiled at his daughter. "If I could lay on the odd headless horseman or chain-rattling specter, I promise you I would."

We might have been forbidden to go into the house next door, but its garden was our special place. Wendy and I often crept through the overgrown shrubbery at the end of the long grass that used to be a lawn, and we used to go right up to the windows and peer into them to see if we could spot any spooks.

"They're friendly ghosts," Wendy
told me as we looked at the house
together. "They wouldn't hurt us.
They'd like to play, if only we could
get in."

One day, Wendy invented the
Sleeping Beauty game.

"Come on, Geejay," she said.
"These thorn bushes and tangled
branches . . . they're the Enchanted
Wood. I'll be the Prince. I have to
cut my way through it so that I can
reach my Princess. She's asleep up
there, can you see? That's her room,

8

that little one, near the roof. You can be my horse. I'm leading you through the wood. It's too overgrown for me to ride, you see."

I didn't particularly like being a horse. I wanted to be the Prince. I thought I'd make a very good Prince because I was brave and fearless, but Wendy was already slashing away at the bushes with an old broom handle she'd found behind the garage door. I followed her. I wanted to get inside No. 1 for reasons of my own that had nothing to do with ghosts. Often when humans leave a place, mice and little birds move in. Unfortunately, even I couldn't find a crack in the door, and all the windows were tightly closed.

"There's no point playing this game anymore," Wendy said. "I'm going over to Lexie's house." Lexie was her friend and lived at No. 27 with Perkins, the oldest of the Cuckoo Square Cats.

After she'd gone, I jumped up onto the sill to see if there was anything tasty running about inside. There

wasn't. The room was dusty, and strips of old wallpaper were peeling off the walls. A few broken chairs lay about in the corners, and the carpets

were torn and moth-eaten. I decided
to go into Cuckoo Square and find
my friends

Perkins,

Blossom,

and Callie,
who I knew would be happy to
see me.

But things were about to change
at No. 1. A few days later, a notice
saying SOLD appeared on the board

outside the house, and Nigel told
us: "A family called Corby have
bought it."

"Have they got any children?"
Wendy wanted to know.

"Have they got any cats?" I said,
meowing loudly, but my family
chose not to listen.

"A son, I think," said Angela. "It'll
be fun, won't it, having new
neighbors?"

2.
My Early Days

I haven't always lived in Cuckoo Square . . . oh, no. I don't like to boast, but I have led a more adventurous life than my friends. Callie, it's true, began her days in a shelter, but as for Blossom and Perkins, they have lived quietly with their families ever since they were kittens. My early days were altogether different. I am by nature a prowler and a growler, a chaser and a racer, and once upon a time I knew danger, and occasional hungry nights. Before I arrived at No. 2, I had another name, and I'd been a stray cat for many months. My first owner was called Ginger, and his hair was exactly the same color as my coat. He lived on a barge on the river with his skinny wife, Milly. They used to call me Lenny.

I often tell my friends stories . . .

sagas of mouse-chasing and bird-
watching;

tales of moonlight meetings with
foxes who didn't realize that a cat
with teeth and claws at the ready
was more than a match for them.

I was feared by many small
animals, all up and down the river,
and I suppose I would have ended
my days there, but Ginger and Milly
grew old and sick and went to live in
a block of flats in the middle of town
where no pets were allowed. They
cried when they parted from me.

"Oh, Lenny," said Milly. "We'll
always remember you. And our
friend Freddy says he'll look after
you as if you were his own child."

So they left me with Freddy. He was kind enough, but he never chatted to me. I was bored. I was lonely. I felt in my whiskers that there were better homes and pleasanter humans somewhere else, and I was right. I left the river and lived as a stray for many weeks. One day, I found myself in Cuckoo Square, and I knew at once that it was a sort of Cat Paradise. Perkins was the first cat I met. When I caught sight of him, he was lying on a bench beside the railings.

"Is there room in this garden for a cat in need of company?" I asked.

Perkins looked at me and said: "There is always a place here in Cuckoo Square for a fine cat like you. Tell me a little about your beginnings."

I settled myself comfortably and told him some of my adventures.

Perhaps I *did* make them a *little* more exciting than they were in real life, but that is what storytelling is about.

When Perkins had heard them, he said: "An adventurous life, to be sure! It comes from living on a river, no doubt. Are you familiar with what the Furry Ancestors have to say on the subject of rivers?"

I had to admit that I was not.

"They say," Perkins went on, "'A river is like the sea in many ways, but it is much longer and thinner and not as salty.' You seem to be a cat of a daring and swashbuckling nature. Your eyes are forever scanning the distant horizon."

"I'm usually looking for something to chase," I said.

"Nevertheless," said Perkins, "you are a wanderer. I'm delighted that your travels have brought you to Cuckoo Square."

It was Blossom who pointed out to me the house that has been my home for more than a year. As soon as Perkins introduced us, she said: "If I were you, I'd try the Saunders family. They live over there at No. 2. The mother and father both work at the library. They used to have a cat, many moons ago, when I was a mere kitten, but she has now gone to join the Furry Ancestors. I know that Wendy, their little girl, would be a good human for any cat. She comes to the square almost every day to talk to us and stroke us."

"She has even," said Callie, "brought us tidbits to eat from time to time."

I took my new friends' advice and made my way to the Saunderses' house. It was quite late in the afternoon, and I was beginning to feel hungry. I sat down near the garage door and began to meow,

trying to sound as pathetic and
plaintive as I could. This was not the
sort of noise I usually made. Since
my early kittenhood, I'd been
perfecting a cry that strikes terror
into the hearts of all small creatures:
furry, flying, and finny. After a
few minutes, a girl came to the
back door.

"Mum," she said. "Dad. Come and see. There's a cat here, and he's beautiful. I love him. Can we keep him? Please?" She came over and knelt down beside me. "You are so beautiful," she said, picking me up and burying her face in my fur. "You are just like a lion, and I love you."

I liked her at once. She was obviously a child of great intelligence and could tell immediately that I was different from other cats.

"How do we know he doesn't belong to someone else?" the girl's mother said. "We'll have to ask all the neighbors if he's theirs before we invite him to live with us."

Wendy looked so sad that I took matters into my own paws and slipped past her and her mother and went into the kitchen. Once I was in, I meowed again, and when a tin of food was put in front of me, I finished it faster than you could twitch your whiskers or whisk your tail.

"See?" Wendy said. "He's starving, poor thing! I think he's come from far, far away. I've never seen him before, and I know all the Cuckoo Square cats. I'm going to call him Ginger Jack."

"Hadn't you better wait," said her mother, "until we're sure he doesn't belong to anybody else? I'll go round the square after supper."

"I *am* sure," said Wendy. "He's ours. You'll see."

She was quite right. Of course, I knew that no one in the square would claim me, so I thought about my new name and decided I liked it. Ginger Jack had a good ring to it. It sounded brave and jaunty and it suited me. I began to purr and in my head I said goodbye to my past life, to the river and the lonely streets of the city, and to my old name. I was a Cuckoo Square Cat now. A different kind of life had begun. The sun was shining on the cushions of the window seat, and they looked so soft and inviting that I settled myself on them for a sleep.

3.
The Corbys Move In

I didn't stay Ginger Jack for very
long. Angela and Nigel Saunders,
Wendy's parents, shortened it to
Geejay almost at once, and that was
what everyone called me, both in
my house and in the square. It was
quicker and easier, and I liked it
because it sounded dashing.

After the SOLD sign appeared on
the board outside No. 1, all of us
cats waited eagerly to see who
would be moving in, and after a few
days, they appeared.

"There they are!" said Callie.
"Aren't they tall and skinny?"

Perkins said: "The man and the woman are tall and skinny. The child is small and skinny. As the Furry Ancestors say: 'Skinny kittens make skinny cats.'"

The Corbys didn't stop to admire the square but shut their front door very firmly behind them.

Wendy saw the family arriving as well. She went into our garden to look over our hedge and see if she could catch sight of the little boy. I slipped between the slats of the fence and into my favorite flower bed

under a particularly leafy bush. I
was enjoying my morning stretch
and scratching my claws along the
trunk of a tree when Mrs. Corby
came running out of the house
waving a broom around and
shouting: "Shoo! Shoo!" at me. I
fled, of course, but not before I'd
given her a good hiss.

She turned to Wendy and said:
"Was that your cat, little girl?"

"Yes," Wendy said. "I'm Wendy Saunders. We're going to be your neighbors. Our cat is called Ginger Jack, but everyone calls him Geejay."

Wendy's mother came out into our garden then, and she and Mrs. Corby made pleasant-sounding human noises at each other.

I thought everything was perhaps going to be all right, and then Mrs. Corby announced: "I would much prefer it if your cat didn't make free with our flower beds. My little boy is allergic to animals."

"I'll try and keep him on this side of the fence," said Angela, "but Geejay is a bit of a wanderer. He has a mind of his own."

Mrs. Corby sniffed and disappeared into the house.

Angela went indoors, too, and then Wendy said: "Look, Geejay, there's the boy, in the window of the living room." She started to wave, and shouted: "Open the window!" over the hedge.

The boy opened the window and leaned out a little.

"Hello," said Wendy. "I'm Wendy. What's your name?"

"Nicky Corby," said the boy. "Do you live next door to us?"

"*You* live next door to *us*," Wendy said, and giggled. "It's a bit difficult talking like this. Why don't you come down and play in my garden? Or I could come to your garden if you like."

"I can't go in the garden. I get ill if I go in the garden. I'm allergic to pollen, and grass and things. I can't help it. I start sneezing and my eyes run, so Mum says I have to stay indoors."

"Come and play in our house, then."

"I can't," Nicky said. "Because of that cat. I'm allergic to fur as well."

"Wow," said Wendy. "Poor old you! But he's not *that cat*. His name is Geejay."

"Will you come and play here?" Nicky asked. "Will you come to tea one day?"

"You ask your mum and I'll ask mine," said Wendy. "Come on, Geejay, let's go and see who's in the square. Bye, Nicky. See you soon."

"See you," said Nicky, and he waved, rather sadly, as we left.

"The Corbys," I announced to my friends after Wendy had gone home, "will not be having any pets. Their son is allergic to fur. I've been asked to stay out of their property."

"Goodness!" said Callie. "What will you do? You love roaming through everyone's back gardens."

"Oh, I'll find a way to stay hidden, never fear. It would take a great deal more than one skinny lady to keep me out of what I have always thought of as my territory."

"Quite right," said Perkins. "The Furry Ancestors say: 'Where the paw has trodden, the paw will always tread.'"

None of us cats could understand how the Corbys could possibly live in a house like No. 1, which seemed to be full of all sorts of people coming and going all the time, with pots of paint and ladders and little portable radios that played loud music. Something that looked like a big metal box with no lid appeared outside the house.

"It is called a skip," said Perkins.
"The humans are transforming their
house, and the skip is to hold
everything they throw away. For my
part, I would wait until everything
was ready before I moved in, but as
the Furry Ancestors say: 'Humans
prepare a house for cats to enjoy.'"

Wendy said: "They're tidying it
up, Geejay. I expect it won't be
haunted anymore."

Vans drove up every day with sofas and chairs and tables, and we cats considered them carefully.

"Those are hard chairs," said Blossom. "I prefer squashy ones myself, full of soft cushions."

There were people in the garden as well, mowing the lawn, cutting the bushes, and, as Wendy said sadly, "spoiling our enchanted wood. We won't be able to play Sleeping Beauty anymore."

Even in *our* garden, it became very hard to take a nap. All day long, men with lawn mowers and hedge trimmers made humming and whizzing noises, and the wilderness disappeared. They attacked every bush and shrub with giant shears, and then they tore out all the undergrowth and took it away in a big truck. Wendy stood with Lexie in our garden and watched as a red-faced man snipped away at some leftover leaves.

"I liked it better before," she said. "It looks quite ordinary now."

4.
Lions!

The day after the Corbys moved in, two strange animals appeared outside No. 1, sitting on either side of the front door.

"What do you think they could be?" Callie asked.

"They're white," said Blossom. "Perhaps they're dogs of some kind

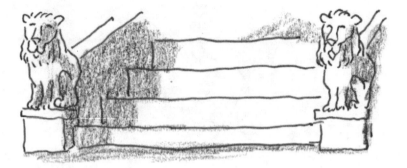

. . . but they are sitting very still, aren't they? Could they be asleep?"

"Those aren't dogs," I said. "They're more like lions, only they're the wrong color."

I knew what lions looked like: exactly like me, only bigger. Every human I'd ever met had told me so.

"Do you think," Callie asked nervously, "that they are friendly?"

"The Furry Ancestors say," Perkins announced, "'Friendly purring makes more friendly purring, but an angry claw causes pain.' Let us introduce ourselves."

"I'm not going on my own," said Blossom. "We should go together."

"They're rather large, though, aren't they?" said Callie. "What if they were to pounce?"

"Geejay and I will go together," said Perkins. "I, after all, am the Senior Cat. You'll come, won't you, Geejay?"

"Of course," I said. "Let's go at once."

Perkins and I crossed over to the Corby house. Perkins hung back a little and let me go first. I didn't mind. I hadn't yet met an animal I was afraid of. When I came close to them, I could see that they were much bigger than I was, but that didn't worry me.

I said: "Welcome, white creatures, to Cuckoo Square. Are you lions? I've been told I look like a lion, so we have something in common."

Silence. The white animals didn't move a whisker. I peered at them more closely.

"Perkins," I said. (He had crept up behind me and was waiting beside the gate.) "These whatever-they-are don't appear to have any whiskers."

I put out a paw and touched one
of them on the foot. It felt like the
pavement. "They're made of stone!"
I said. "They're not alive. They
couldn't talk to us even if they
wanted to."

"Goodness!" said Perkins. "What
funny people these Corbys must be,
to have pets made out of stone."

Later on, when Wendy came back
from school, she said: "Stone lions!
How posh! The Corbys are trying to
impress us, putting statues by their

door." She disappeared into No. 2.

"It seems," I said to my friends, "that having statues beside your door impresses people and is a Good Thing. Perhaps we should do it for our humans."

"Would we have to stay very still?" Blossom asked.

"Oh, yes," I said. "If we're to look like proper statues."

"It sounds rather boring to me," said Blossom, "and Miles will wonder why I haven't come in for my tea. Perkins will sit with you, I'm sure."

"Nothing I'd like better," said Perkins, "but alas, it is time for my nap. I think I will leave being a statue for some other day. But you go ahead, Geejay, if you feel you must."

"Callie?" I said, although I knew that she would never agree to sit outside for such a long time. Buggins, the little black kitten who had come to share her house, would appear from out of nowhere as he always did, and jump up and tickle her nose with his.

"I'm sorry, Geejay," she said. "I have to go and find Buggins. He's disappeared again. It's very hard to keep an eye on him."

I was just about to sit down next to the stone lions when Wendy came out to find me.

"Come on, Geejay," she said. "The boy next door is looking out of one of the windows at the back. Let's go and talk to him."

I followed her round to the garden. I would have to leave being posh and impressive for another day.

No. 1 Cuckoo Square was
beginning to look very spick and
span, but there were still small piles
of bricks lying in the path, and men
in overalls still came and went
carrying pots of paint and ladders.

Wendy was very excited. She was
going to tea the next day with
Nicky Corby.

"Such a shame you can't come too, Geejay. Never mind . . . I'll tell you all about it when I get back."

Another cat would have been happy to curl up and go to sleep until she returned, but not me! I wanted to get into that house and see what it was like. I wanted to be invited in, like Wendy, but I hadn't been, so I decided to sneak into the house first, all by myself. This should have been easy, but it wasn't. Every door seemed to be shut, and not one single window was open.

Just as I was losing heart, Mrs. Corby came out onto the front steps and said to one of the men busily painting the outside of the house: "I'm sure these lions shouldn't stay here while you're working. They're bound to get spots of paint all over them. Perhaps you'd be kind enough to help me carry them inside."

This was my chance! I immediately took up my position on the steps, next to one of the stone creatures. I sat as stiff and straight as I could, and waited for the man to pick me up and bring me inside with the stone lions. Amazingly, he just smiled at me and said: "Sorry, me old alley cat . . . only posh stone lions in here. Mrs. C. says so."

I made my way to Cuckoo Square, where my friends were waiting.

"He called me an alley cat," I said. "I can't imagine why he didn't think I was a lion too. I've been told I look just like one."

"And so you do," said Blossom soothingly. "Never mind, Wendy will tell you all about tea at No. 1 when she's been. And all about Nicky and his parents."

"I'm not giving up," I told her. "I'm going to get in there one day, you'll see."

"I'm sure you will," said Callie. "You can do everything."

Callie is a very sensible cat in many ways.

5.

Inside No. 1

The following evening, as soon as
Wendy came home, she went over to
Nicky's house. I watched her
shutting the front door behind her
and began to think of all sorts of
ways that I might creep into No. 1.
First, I went down the path at the
side of the house and jumped up

onto the windowsill of the kitchen.
There were Wendy and Nicky,
sitting at the table, having their tea.
In our house, there were open
notebooks and old newspapers on
the table, but Mrs. Corby had cups
and saucers with roses on them, and
the children were eating tiny little
sandwiches and iced cakes.

Wendy saw me looking in, but I
jumped down at once. I didn't want
Nicky to see me and tell his mother.

I made my way to
the big tree that
still stood near the
house, and started to
climb. I'm a good
climber, and soon I
was on one of the
highest branches,
peering in through
the window of one of the bedrooms.
Unfortunately, the room I was
looking into had Mrs. Corby in it,
and she opened the window to
shout at me.

"Scat!" she cried.
"Get down
from that tree
this instant. . . .
Go on.
Scram!"

It's always hard to run down a tree in a dignified fashion, but I did my best. I even forgot to hiss at Mrs. Corby. Never mind, I told myself. I shall have my revenge!

I crept along the ground to one of the flower beds and dug a small hole in it. That was so enjoyable that I dug another in another place, and then a few more. Soon, all the soft earth in two long flower beds was filled with little holes. I was getting ready to make some more when a squirrel decided to skitter down from one of the trees. If there's one thing I can't resist, it's a squirrel chase. Off across the lawn we ran, in and out of the trees at the bottom of the garden, up into the lowest branches, and away across the back patio. One hardly ever catches a squirrel, in my experience, but this doesn't matter, because they are not the tastiest of animals.

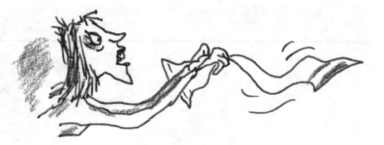

Mrs. Corby came out to see what all the rushing about was. She was flapping a dish towel in front of her face. "Shoo," she cried. "I thought I told you to stay in your own garden."

Then she caught sight of the holes and began to shriek: "Oh, you naughty cat . . . go away! Go on. And don't dare to let me find you in this garden again . . . or else . . . SHOO!"

I fled, and went in search of the other Cuckoo Square Cats.

"Mrs. Corby at No. 1," I told them, "is not a lady to start a fight with. Have you come across her?"

Not one of them had.

"My advice to you," I continued, "is to stay away. That garden is a dangerous place. She came after me with all sorts of weapons."

"Will *you* stay away?" Callie asked.

"Certainly not," I said. "That's *my* garden. After all, I was there long before the Corbys were. *They* haven't marked every single tree, have they?"

My friends agreed with me.

I said: "And I'll tell you something else. I'll get into the house, too. You'll see."

★ ★ ★

From that day on, I was on the
lookout. I watched the house,
waiting for my chance. One day, I
knew, someone would leave a door
open, or forget to close a window,
and then I would pounce.

"Look!" said Blossom one
afternoon. "The door is open at
No. 1."

"Thank you, Blossom," I said. "I'd just noticed it myself."

I hadn't noticed it. I had been asleep, dreaming of hunting beside the moonlit river of my kittenhood, but I didn't want to admit it. Heroes are not supposed to sleep. Neither are hunters. I padded across the road. Cuckoo Square was deserted.

The men with the ladders and the paint pots had moved to the back of the house. I could hear loud music coming from their radios as I ran up the front steps. Blossom was right. The door *was* open. I took a deep breath and put my head round it.

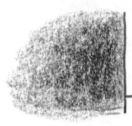

The hall was quite empty. A blink of the eye and a whisk of the tail, and there I was: inside No. 1 at last. I wished my friends could have seen me. I was rubbing my chin along the leg of the hall table when I heard Mrs. Corby's voice and flattened myself against the wall.

"I can see you in the mirror," she
said from inside the downstairs
cloakroom, where she was up on a
stepladder, fixing a new light fitting
to the ceiling. "I thought I told you
that you weren't allowed in this
house. You are the most disobedient
cat I've ever seen. Shoo!"

69

She started to climb down the ladder, and just at that moment a draft of wind came whistling round the front door, and the door of the little room slammed shut.

"Open this door at once, someone!" Mrs. Corby shouted, banging on the wood. "I can't get out . . . the whole door handle's come away in my hand. Who was supposed to fit this doorknob? Help! Someone come and let me out NOW!"

Nobody came. The workmen at the back of the house with their radios on certainly couldn't hear her, and I knew that there was no window in the downstairs cloakroom of this house because it was just like ours. But Nicky was in. Surely he could hear her? Why hadn't *he* come rushing downstairs to help his mother? The same thought must have occurred to Mrs. Corby.

"Help!" she called. "Nicky! Help! How am I going to get out of here? Drat this old house! Nicky! Why don't you come down? I know you're in your room. Oh dear," Mrs. Corby moaned.

I knew that our house would be empty for a long time. Wendy was going to tea with Lexie, and Angela and Nigel came home quite late sometimes. Mrs. Corby went on banging on the door and shouting.

I knew exactly what I had to do. It was up to me to save the day and go and find Nicky. I ran upstairs and began looking for him. I found his room at last, on the top floor. The door was open. I ran in and jumped up onto the table. Nicky

was wearing earphones and playing
a game on a computer exactly like
Wendy's.

"Geejay!" he said, and took the
earphones off. "What are you doing
here? My mum'll be furious. How did
you get in?"

73

I meowed as loudly as I could, jumped down to the floor, and pushed at Nicky's legs with my chin.

He didn't move. I took one of his shoelaces between my teeth and pulled.

"Stop it!" said Nicky. "Why are you pulling me? What do you want me to do?" I ran to the door and then back to him, trying to make him see what I wanted him to do.

"Your mother," I told him, "has shut herself in the downstairs cloakroom by accident. Come downstairs. Come downstairs now!"

I don't know how long it would have taken him to understand me, but luckily Mrs. Corby's voice came floating up through the house just at that moment.

"Nicky!" She sounded very far away. "Help! Help!"

"Mum!" Nicky shouted, and then he picked me up. "Where is she? Why is she calling out like that? Come on, she's in trouble. You were trying to tell me, weren't you? Let's go and have a look."

Before I knew what was happening, we were dashing downstairs together.

"Mum!" he cried. "Where are you? What's the matter?"

Mrs. Corby's voice sounded muffled through the door. "I'm in here. . . . I'm stuck. The handle's fallen off on this side. Can you open it from your side?"

"Yes," said Nicky. He put me down on the hall carpet and opened the door.

"You took your time," she said. "Where on earth were you?"

"I was upstairs. I had my earphones on. If it hadn't been for Geejay, you could have been locked in there till Dad came home, or at least till Mr. Perry came in for some tea."

"We'll discuss the cat later. . . ."

"Geejay," said Nicky. "Not *the cat*. He's got a name. He came all the way upstairs to get me. He's a hero." Nicky picked me up again and began to cuddle me, burying his nose in my fur.

"STOP!" Mrs. Corby yelled. "Put that animal down at once! You're allergic to cats."

"Am I?" Nicky sniffed the air. "No, I'm not. Really. Look, I'm fine. Isn't that great? It's brilliant. I love this cat!"

"Nicky," said Mrs. Corby. "Could we discuss cats and your allergies some other time? I'm going to find Mr. Perry this minute and get him to fix this door handle at once, before anyone else gets locked in. In fact, you can go and fetch him for me. I need a cup of tea. My nerves are all of a jangle. . . ."

Nicky went. I sat down and looked at Mrs. Corby from a safe distance. In my opinion, she should have said something . . . apologized for chasing me and being so rude to me so many times . . . but she went off to the kitchen and left me alone in the hall.

I made my way out of the front door. I wanted to tell my friends about my adventures in what was, after all, Enemy Territory. As I passed the stone lions, I couldn't resist boasting. I said: "You might be posh and made of stone, but *I* am a hero! Nicky said so."

They said nothing, of course, but they didn't look too happy.

6.
A Happy Ending

The children were sitting in Nicky's
room. I was there with them,
because ever since my heroic rescue
of Mrs. Corby and the discovery
that Nicky didn't sneeze and
wheeze whenever he came near me,
she had allowed me into her house.
The doctors had said Nicky might

grow out of his allergies, and he had. Still, she wasn't exactly welcoming. There were no little tidbits, such as I was given when I visited Perkins's house, or Blossom's, or Callie's, and she would never be the sort of person who stroked me as she passed.

"So why," said Wendy to Nicky, "did anyone think you were allergic to cats?"

"I had a puppy when I was little. We lived in the country then. I got him for my birthday, and he was the best present I ever had. I loved him. He had floppy brown ears. But after he'd been with us for a few days, I got really wheezy and it felt sore when I breathed, so poor little Billy had to be taken to an animal shelter for rehoming. I cried and cried. I was so sad. I can still remember how sad I felt."

I couldn't imagine anyone being so upset about a puppy with floppy brown ears, but it *is* true that there are humans who are very fond of dogs.

"Well, you can have a pet again now," Wendy said. "I'd get a cat, like

Geejay, who's a real hero, but you could get another puppy if you wanted, couldn't you?"

The fur on the back of my neck stood up. Was there really going to be a *dog* living next door? That would make life very difficult for me. I am not particularly fond of dogs.

"No," said Nicky. "My mum doesn't want to do all the walking. And she says dogs like the country better than the town. I want a cat."

"Come and see the other Cuckoo Square Cats," said Wendy, and she and Nicky went downstairs. I followed them to the square.

Perkins, Blossom, and Callie were all sitting near the railings. Wendy told Nicky their names, and he stroked them and chatted to them.

"I'm going to ask my mum if I can have a cat of my own," he said.

"That's a brilliant idea," said Wendy. "He can be a friend for Geejay and the other Cuckoo Square cats."

I looked at my friends.

"I don't know how easy it will be to persuade Mrs. Corby that she should share her house with one of us," I said. "She is *not* a natural animal lover."

"The Furry Ancestors say," said Perkins, "'It takes a cat to make a cat lover,' so perhaps there is hope."

Wendy and Nicky walked round the square.

"You can come and play in my house tomorrow," Wendy said. "Now that you're not allergic anymore, you can go anywhere. We'll play Princes and Princesses. You can be the Prince."

They went back to Nicky's house, and I stayed in the square with my friends.

"I thought *you* were the Prince in Wendy's games," said Blossom. "Aren't you cross?"

"No," I said. "I could never be cross with Wendy. She called me a hero. So did Nicky. Being a hero is just as good as being a prince."

All the Cuckoo Square Cats purred in agreement.

About the Author

Adèle Geras has published more than eighty acclaimed books for children and young adults, including *My Grandmother's Stories,* which won the Sydney Taylor Award in 1991. Her most recent novel is *Troy,* which was a *Boston Globe–Horn Book* Honor Book She is married, has two grown-up daughters, and lives in Manchester, England. She loves books, movies, all kinds of theater, and, of course, cats.

About the Illustrator

Tony Ross is the award-winning illustrator of several books for children, including the Amber Brown series by Paula Danziger. He lives with his family in Cheshire, England.